Henry and Mudge and the Big Sleepover

The Twenty-Eighth Book of Their Adventures

by Cynthia Rylant

illustrated by Suçie Stevenson

Ready-to-Read

Simon Spotlight
New York London Toronto Sydney

THE HENRY AND MUDGE BOOKS

Simon Spotlight
An imprint of Simon & Schuster Children's Publishing Division
1230 Avenue of the Americas, New York, NY 10020
Text copyright © 2006 by Cynthia Rylant
Illustrations copyright © 2006 by Suçie Stevenson
Also available in a Simon & Schuster Books for Young Readers hardcover edition.
Designed by Lucy Ruth Cummins
The text of this book was set in 18-point Goudy.
The illustrations were rendered in pen-and-ink and watercolor
Manufactured in the United States of America
First Aladdin Paperbacks edition May 2007
20 19 18 17 16 15 14 13 12
The Library of Congress has cataloged the hardcover edition as follows:
Rylant, Cynthia.
Henry and Mudge and the big sleepover: the twenty-eighth book of their adventures / story by
Cynthia Rylant; pictures by Suçie Stevenson.
p. cm. — (The Henry and Mudge books)
Summary: Henry and his dog Mudge are invited to a sleepover in Patrick's attic, where they watch
monster movies, eat pizza, and enjoy a contest to determine whose dog is the best popcorn catcher.
[1. Sleepovers—Fiction. 2. Dogs—Fiction. 3.] I. Stevenson, Suçie, ill. II. Title.
PZ7.R982Heak 2006
[Fic.]—dc 21
98-020935
ISBN-13: 978-0-689-81171-5 (hc.)
ISBN-10: 0-689-81171-3 (hc.)
ISBN-13: 978-0-689-83451-6 (pbk.)
ISBN-10: 0-689-83451-9 (pbk.)
1011 LAK

Contents

Raining Popcorn!

Henry and Henry's big dog, Mudge, were playing outside one day when Henry got a phone call. It was Henry's friend, Patrick.

"I'm having a sleepover Saturday night,"
said Patrick.
"Can you and Mudge come?"
Henry's mother said yes.

"We'll be there!" said Henry.

Patrick told Henry to bring a pillow,
a sleeping bag, and a flashlight.
"Cool!" said Henry.

"And don't forget Mudge," said Patrick.
Henry would never forget Mudge.

"We're going to a sleepover, Mudge,"
said Henry.
Mudge wagged.
"We'll stay up late," said Henry.
Mudge wagged again.

"And watch monster movies," Henry said.
Mudge wagged some more.

"And eat lots of popcorn," said Henry.
Mudge jumped up and did a little dance.
Next to crackers, popcorn was Mudge's
favorite food.
He liked to catch it in the air.

"It will be *raining* popcorn, Mudge!"
said Henry.
Flashlights, monster movies, and popcorn.
Henry could hardly wait for Saturday.

11

Bouncy

When Henry and Mudge got to Patrick's
house on Saturday, the living room was full of
boys and dogs.
Everyone was bouncy.

13

The boys were bouncy.

The dogs were bouncy.

Patrick's parents looked nervous.

They had a *million* knickknacks.

"Everybody to the attic!" said Patrick's father, catching a knickknack in the air.

16

Henry and Mudge followed everybody
to the attic.

It was ENORMOUS!

"Wow!" said Henry.

"It's like a ship!"

The boys and dogs got bouncy again.
"Have fun!" said Patrick's father with
a big smile.

20 (There wasn't a knickknack in sight.)

He closed the door, and the sleepover began.

Giant Lizards

Patrick had lots of games for the boys to play.

There were board games and video games.

There were little baskets and little balls.

There was even a small bowling game. 23

But no one could play it because a bulldog
kept taking the pins.

When it got dark, Patrick's mother brought pizza, and the monster movies began.

The boys and dogs ate pizza and watched giant lizards eat entire towns.

"Mudge would be a good monster," said
one boy.
Henry shook his head.

"No," said Henry
"He'd just kiss everybody."
Mudge wagged and kissed the piece of pizza in
Henry's hand.

When the movies were over, the boys had a
popcorn contest for the dogs.
The dog who was the best popcorn catcher
would win.
Henry was sure Mudge would be the winner.

But he wasn't!
A poodle who did backflips to catch her
pieces won.

Henry didn't mind, though.
Mudge was still the only dog who could eat a
whole bowl of popcorn in one bite!

31

In the Bag

The boys played more games, then finally it
was sleeping bag time.

The boys got into their bags with their dogs.

(Mudge couldn't fit in Henry's bag, so he had
his own.)

The boys turned on their flashlights and made
silly shadows on the wall.
One boy made a kitty, and all of the dogs
barked and barked and barked.
The boys laughed forever.

Then, somehow, the night finally grew quiet.
Everyone fell asleep.

Back home the next day, Henry told his parents about the sleepover.

"Mudge was the best dog there," said Henry.

"He was?" said Henry's mother.

"Yes," said Henry.

"Because in the morning, all the dogs were in
his sleeping bag!
And he didn't even mind!"

40